The Wild Explorers

LORRAINE LAWRANCE

Contents

Funny Bodies

My reading goal ★ Talk about the meaning of words and illustrations with others.

What is your favourite hobby? Mine is keeping a **record** of the strange things that my body does.

You're <u>off</u> <u>your rocker!</u>

Go on, my son!

You're <u>as</u> <u>nutty as a</u> <u>fruit cake.</u>

I'm sure you have wondered why sometimes you get sick in your mouth, right?

Have you ever thought about why our teeth fall out, why onions make us cry and why we have slimy green things up our nose?

Let's find out why our bodies **behave** in the ways they do.

What is a booger?

A booger is a sticky, slimy green glop that lives up your nose.

It is very useful, <u>believe it or not</u>.

It keeps your nose **moist** and it warms the air you breathe.

It also **protects** your lungs. The air we breathe has dust, germs and **allergens**, such as pollen, in it.

If all this reached our lungs, it could make them sore and red or **infected**. Boogers trap a lot of this dust and dirt before it gets there.

Tiny hairs in our nose help move it to the front of our nostrils.
It comes out as a booger when we sneeze, blow or pick our nose.

Germs

Dust

Tiny hairs

Pollen and
other allergens

Stop

Nostrils

What you do with it then is up to you,
but <u>bear this in mind</u>: some say that
eating boogers is good for you! I am
not **convinced**.

Did you know? The speed of a
sneeze is approximately 100 mph.
That's faster than a cheetah can run!

Why do we get sick?

Puking, barfing, vomiting, **up-chucking** – there are not many things worse than getting sick.

If it is that nasty, then why do we do it?

It is our body's clever way of helping us and protecting us.

Sometimes germs and bugs can reach our stomach. This can happen when we <u>come into contact with</u> a vomiting bug or gone-off food.

When this happens, our body wants to get rid of the bugs quickly. This is done by puking them up.

Oh, you know those bits of orange that we see in our sick? They are not carrots! Doctors say that the orange stuff is the **lining** of our stomach, that comes up with the food. Nice!

Why do onions make us cry?

It's a strange one! I'm sure most people don't feel sad when **slicing** up an onion.

We don't cry when cutting up a carrot. So why does chopping an onion make us cry <u>buckets of tears</u>?

Onions contain a **chemical** (kem-i-kal). This chemical makes our eyes red and itchy. When an onion is cut, the chemical comes out of the onion. It then enters our eyes.

Our **tear ducts** (the holes in the small red triangles at the corners of your eyes) then make tears to **flush** out the chemical and clean our eyes.

Why do we have two sets of teeth?

Pearly whites, **gnashers**, fangs, tusks, choppers and prongs are just some of the words people have for teeth.

Have you ever wondered why we have two sets of teeth, but not two sets of anything else? It's **bizarre**!

Imagine if your baby eyes fell out. Imagine you had to put them under your pillow for the Eye Fairy, before waiting for your adult eyes to grow. That just wouldn't happen.

So why does it happen with our teeth?

A baby's jaw is too small to fit the number of teeth we need as an adult. You see, a baby has 20 teeth, but an adult has 32 teeth.

These 12 extra teeth can only come through when our jaws have grown to a **certain** size. This is why our teeth begin to fall out at the age of six. Most people have all of their adult teeth by the age of 13.

The Biggest Burp Ever
by Kenn Nesbitt

The record, so far, for the world's biggest burp,
is held by Belinda Melinda McNurp.
It wasn't on purpose. She wasn't to blame.
Her tummy just rumbled, and out the burp came.

Belinda then instantly saw her mistake.
The ground began trembling and starting to shake.
That rumble was suddenly more of a roar.
It busted the windows and knocked down the door.

Her mother and father both covered their ears.
Her brother and sister were nearly in tears.
Her puppy looked panicked and yipped as he fled.
Her kitten just cowered and covered his head.

The cars on the street began skidding and stopping.
The shoppers in shops started dropping their shopping.
The squirrels all burrowed. The birds flew away.
The sun disappeared for the rest of the day

as clouds began thundering all around town.
The trees toppled over. The buildings fell down.
Tornadoes and hurricanes blew through the sky.
The rivers flowed backward. The oceans ran dry.

Volcanoes erupted from Perth to Peru.
The Grand Canyon widened. Mount Everest grew.
The Earth started spinning a different direction.
And, worst of all, I lost my iPhone connection.

Belinda was pretty embarrassed alright,
but she was well-mannered, and very polite.
And that's why she knew it would all be okay
when she said, "Excuse me," and went on her way.

To the Art Exhibition ☞

My reading goal ★ Learn new words and read them on my own.

Ella has started art classes.

Lainey and Ava from Ella's street go too. The **trio** became the best of buds over the summer. They **attend** classes every Tuesday after school. Their mams take turns to drop and collect them.

Miss Evelyn is their art teacher. She is from Spain. She is very creative. The girls like her a lot.

Miss Evelyn is going to **display** their work in the Crawford Art Gallery soon. The artists will explain their work to the **viewers**. It's a bit like show and tell. Here is a sneak preview!

Papier Mâché

I want to explain how *papier mâché* works.

What is *papier mâché*?

'*Papier mâché*' is French for 'chewed paper'. It is **construction** art. Construction art is when you make things using **materials**.

> Materials are things like newspaper, cardboard boxes, toilet-roll holders, pipe cleaners and milk carton tops.

Papier mâché uses **layers** of newspaper. The layers are **bound** together by paste to make an object.

  Warning: *Papier mâché* can be very messy.

Did you know? Even though *papier mâché* is a French name, it came from China, where paper was invented.

How does it work?

To construct something, you have to make a form.

The form is the main part or the body. You can see below that the form used is a balloon. You can make a form using balloons, paper rolls, plastic bottles, paper cups or egg cartons. You can change the shape of your form by sticking other materials onto it.

Milk carton tops and egg cartons were stuck onto the balloon to make an animal shape.

Paste is something that makes things stick together. You can use it to stick paper, cardboard, wallpaper, **fabric**, plastic, etc.

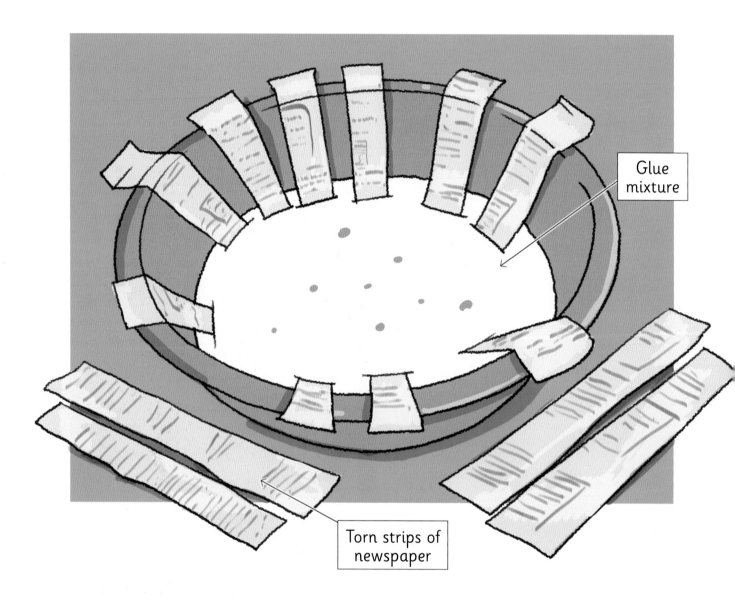

Glue mixture

Torn strips of newspaper

Torn newspaper strips work better than cut strips. They make the **object** look smoother.

If you mix too much water or too much glue, then it will not stick.

It is important to dip one strip of newspaper at a time into the paste. If you did a few layers at a time, it would get lumpy.

Overlap the strips on the balloon.

> To **overlap** means to lay the strips in different directions over each other. Overlapping the strips will make the form stronger.

Look at the images below. Can you explain what is happening?

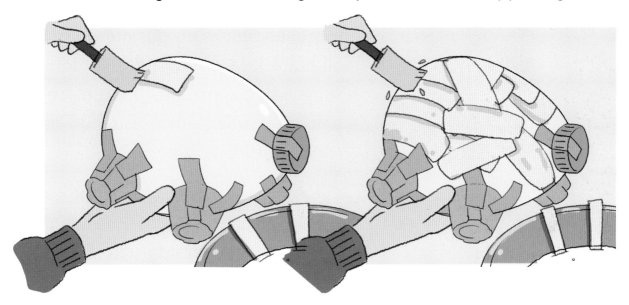

It is important to let the form dry before adding another layer. You need to **apply** at least two or three layers.

> Layers make the form more solid. If you do not have enough layers, you will be able to see through to the form. If you have too many layers, it will look too **bulky**.

Once the form is dry, you can **decorate** it. Can you describe how ours looks?

Marbling

I would like to explain how marbling works.

What is marbling?

Marbling is creating patterns using oil paint.

How does marbling work?

Marbling works by putting a little oil paint into a tub and then adding some white spirit into the tub. The paint is thinned down using an old spoon until it is watery.

⚠ Warning: White spirit can be dangerous. You must ask an adult to help you if you want to try marbling at home.

Warning: Marbling should be done in an airy room. Keep the windows and doors open.

If the paint is too thick, it will not spread out nicely. If you add too much white spirit, the paint will become too watery. This is why it is important to follow the instructions carefully.

Half-fill a tray with water. You can use a spoon to place some of the thinned oil paint onto the water in the tray. Use as many colours as you wish.

When water and oil mix, the oil floats to the top. You can make shapes in the oil paint.

Using the tail-end of a spoon, mix the colours together to get a swirly pattern. By floating paper on top of the design, it **transfers** onto the paper.

Marbling came from Japan. It is called *suminagashi* or 'ink floating'.

Paper People

I would like to explain how to make paper people.

After cutting out the body parts, you can use paper **fasteners** to **attach** each body part.

What are paper people?

Paper people are people that are made out of paper.

How do paper people work?

To make paper people, you need to be good at drawing the parts of the body. It is important that the lines and shapes in your drawings are **symmetrical**.

Did you ever do an art lesson at school in which you placed paint in the middle of a page and then folded it over to make a butterfly with two **equal** parts? That's symmetry!

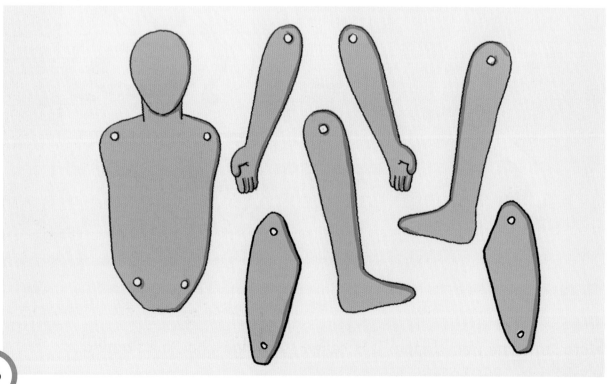

Paper fasteners are small, round metal objects. They have two **spiky** bits at the back. The spiky bits pierce through paper. They fold back at the other side to keep the paper together.

Paper fasteners will allow the body parts to move and swing about. They need to be placed where the shoulders meet the arms and where the hips meet the legs.

If you tape a piece of string to the head and another piece to the arms and legs, it will make the arms and legs move.

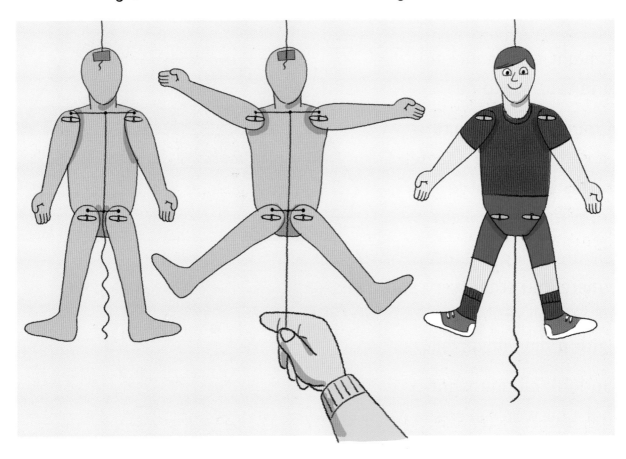

What could you use to decorate your paper person?

Did you know? Historians use paper people to show how people dressed long ago.

So, what do you think? *Papier mâché*, marbling and paper people are only a <u>taster</u> of what is on show on the night. Why not come along and learn some more?

Nate the Creative

by Kenn Nesbitt

I'm Nate the Creative
and here's what I do:
I wake up each day and
create something new.

I might bake a pickle
and skyscraper pie.
I might take a nickel
and teach it to fly.

I might paint a picture
of checkerboard cheese,
or fashion a statue
from typewriter keys.

Or dream up a dance
where you stand very still,
or buy all of France
with a nine-dollar bill.

So look all you want
but you won't ever see
a person on earth
as creative as me.

Tomorrow, I might make
a hat out of you.
I'm Nate the Creative.
It's just what I do.

On Friday, Ella and Tom went on a nature walk with their class. They went to Doneraile National Park. They travelled by bus with their packed lunches and their raincoats (just <u>to be on the safe side</u>). They sang songs all the way.

The park is famous for its **wildlife**. It has information signs **scattered** all around.

Ms Carol made a **worksheet** for the children to do in groups as they made their way around. Each group was also given a camera and an empty bag for **gathering** things.

19

Here is what they learned:

Why are trees important?	Why does a tree shed its leaves?
They clean the air. They give us **oxygen**. They are home for many creatures. They can be used to make paper, tools and homes.	A **deciduous** tree sheds its leaves once a year. It has wide leaves that can easily be damaged by **harsh** winter weather. The tree **sheds** its leaves to protect itself.
Take a photo of a deciduous tree.	**Label the parts of the tree.**
	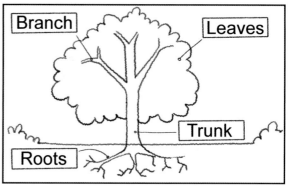
Make a rubbing of the bark on the trunk of the tree.	**Explain how it works.**
	The paper is something to make the print on. The bark is the thing that will be printed. The crayon is the thing that will create the print.

You can tell how old a tree is by counting the rings in its trunk. Tree trunks grow thicker every year by adding one new ring.

The trunk of the tree is protected by the layer of bark. Trees can live for thousands of years.

Gather some leaves and put them in your bag.
Examine the leaves and label them.

Elder

Lime

Hawthorn

Beech

Silver Birch

Horse Chestnut

Sycamore

Field Maple

Oak

Hazel

Willow

Rowan

Why do animals hibernate and what do they do when they hibernate?

Animals **hibernate** so that they can save their energy and **survive** the cold winter months. They sleep for long periods of time. They eat lots of food during autumn. They store it in their bodies so that they do not have to wake up to eat while they are resting.

Take photos of the animals you meet along the walk.

Rabbit

Squirrel

Fox

Hedgehog

Field mouse

Bat

What sound does a hedgehog make?

A hedgehog makes **grunting** noises, which is why it is called a hedge 'hog'. (A hog is a pig.)

What is a hedgehog covered in?

Except for its face, legs and belly, a hedgehog is covered with **prickly** spines.

How does a hedgehog protect itself?

It can curl into a tight ball and tuck in its head, tail and legs. It does this to protect the parts of its body that do not have stiff, sharp spines.

What does a hedgehog like to eat?

A hedgehog likes to eat insects, mice, snails, lizards, frogs, eggs and even snakes!

Then, the class went on a bug hunt.

Check off all the bugs you can find.

Butterfly ☐	Ant ☐	Bee ☐
Dragonfly ☐	Moth ☐	Caterpillar ☐
Beetle ☐	Ladybird ☐	Grasshopper ☐
Woodlouse ☐	Fly ☐	Centipede ☐

Explain how grasshoppers make sounds.

Male grasshoppers make a singing sound by rubbing a back leg against one of their hard front wings. The **rough** leg makes the wing **vibrate** and make a sound.
It is like a bow playing a **cello**.

Did you know?

Lots of people in African countries eat moths. They are packed with **protein** and healthy fats. These creatures have some very important **minerals** in them, such as calcium, zinc and iron.

Aithníonn ciaróg ciaróg eile!
A beetle recognises another beetle

- An adult beetle has two sets of wings.
- The female beetle lays hundreds of eggs.
- Most beetles live for only a year.
- Beetles cannot see very well, so they communicate using sounds.
- Ladybirds are beetles and are thought to bring good luck in many countries.
- Fireflies are also beetles. They glow in the dark to communicate.

The class had a very active and interesting nature walk.

Tom's favourite part was examining all of the different bugs with a **magnifying** glass. Ella's favourite part was collecting up all the different types of leaves. What was yours?

Come, Little Leaves

by George Cooper

"Come, little leaves,"
Said the wind one day,
"Come to the meadows
With me and play;
Put on your dresses
Of red and gold,
For summer is gone,
And the days grow cold."

Soon as the leaves
Heard the wind's loud call,
Down they came fluttering,
One and all.
Over the meadows
They danced and flew,
All singing the soft
Little songs they knew.

My Little Book of Calm

4

My reading goal ★ Share my thoughts and opinions about this text with others.

Ella is a strong, healthy, happy girl. Most of the time she feels happy. Every now and then she feels sad.

Sometimes, she gets <u>butterflies in her tummy</u> and feels a bit shaky. Sometimes, she starts to worry. It can start over a test at school, over something someone said or because of something new she is going to do. This is normal. It happens to everyone.

Ella has been learning about how to be **aware** of how she is feeling. This is called being **mindful**.

How Does Mindfulness Work?

You can start by <u>paying attention</u> to your breathing.

> Deep breathing makes more oxygen go to your brain. This helps your body to feel calm.

<u>Take a deep breath</u>. Breathe in through your nose and out through your mouth.

Feel your belly rise as you breathe in and go down as you breathe out.

> When you breathe in, you **inhale**. When you breathe out, you **exhale**.

Now take a deeper breath.

> Deep breathing helps to slow down your heart rate. This helps to relax your body.

Rest in the space between the breaths. This still, quiet place is always with us, whether we're sad, angry, worried, excited or happy.

Using your **inner voice**, ask yourself how you are feeling right now. Why are you feeling this way? What has happened during the day to make you feel this way?

You are now aware of what you are feeling and thinking.

I am feeling a little bit worried. This is not something that will last forever. I know that this feeling will **pass**. I remember how it was to feel calm. I remember to practise my belly breathing. I am strong. I am healthy. I am in **control**.

Ella's Top Tips

1. Keep it simple.

Notice your thoughts. Notice how your body feels. Notice what your ears are hearing.

By noticing what you are thinking, feeling and hearing, you begin to <u>tune into</u> yourself.

You are not thinking about other things.

You are not thinking about other people.

You are noticing you.

Breathe.

2. Pay attention to what you can hear.

You could use a bell, a set of **chimes** or a phone app that has water, wind or other gentle sounds on it.

Sounds like these can help you to relax.

They can help you to imagine a quiet, calm place.

You might feel so relaxed that you <u>drift off to sleep</u>.

Breathe.

3. Create a mindful bedtime routine.

<u>Take the weight off your shoulders</u> before you go to sleep.

Close your eyes and bring your **attention** to your toes, then to your feet, then to your legs, etc.

Feel each body part melt into the **mattress**.

This helps to relax your body at the end of the day.

Breathe.

Right foot, left foot. Right ankle and calf, left ankle and calf. Right knee, left knee. Right thigh, left thigh, both feet and legs. Hips, bum, belly, **entire** lower body. Chest and heart. Right arm, left arm. Right hand, left hand. Shoulders, neck, face. Whole body at once.

4. Practise with a breathing buddy.

Grab a stuffed animal and lie down on your back with your buddy on your belly.

Focus your attention on the <u>rise and fall</u> of the stuffed animal as you breathe in and out.

Breathe.

5. Make your walks mindful.

Take a 'noticing walk'.

Stroll through your neighbourhood and notice things you have not seen before. Be silent and pay attention to all of the sounds you can hear, such as animals, birds or a lawnmower.

Breathe.

6. Check your personal weather report.

Think of the weather report that best describes your feelings at this very **moment** – sunny, rainy, stormy, calm or windy.

You can't change the weather outside, but you can change how you **react** to how you are feeling.

Breathe.

7. Practise mindful eating.

Think about how the food you choose to eat **affects** your body.

Healthy food will make you feel fresher and give you more energy. Unhealthy food can make you feel **sluggish** and sickly.

Enjoy the food you eat. Learn to taste food. Enjoy the sweet, **savoury** and spicy tastes.

Breathe.

8. Stay active.

Don't be a <u>couch potato</u>.

Staying active is something the whole family can do.

Whatever kind of activity you like to do, do it!

Ella enjoys yoga. It helps to **strengthen** the body and helps to keep you **balanced**.

Breathe.

Breathe and Be
by Kate Coombs

I breathe slowly in,
I breathe slowly out. My breath
is a river of peace.
I am here in the world.
Each moment I can breathe
and be.

There's a quiet place
in my head like an egg hidden
in a nest. A place
I go when the world is loud.
A moss-green forest with birds.

How I rush rush rush!
Thoughts flutter and dart like birds.
Slow down, thoughts.
Come quietly with me.
There is time to breathe and be.

I watch the stream.
Each thought is a floating leaf.
One leaf is worry,
another leaf is sadness.
The leaves drift slowly away.

A Day in the Life of Tom's Shoe

5

My reading goal ★ Talk about the imaginative parts of this text.

Today was just <u>one of those days</u> – one of those days that you'd rather forget! I knew it was going to be bad from the minute I woke up. For starters, I had a terrible night's sleep.

After training last night, Tom did not place me nicely on the shoe rack as he has been told to do many, many times. Oh no! He kicked me off and I landed upside down on the cold kitchen floor, where I've been freezing from heel to toe all night!

Mind you, that was **bliss** compared to the rest of the day.

When I saw Tom coming to get me, I couldn't believe my eyes. He was wearing the same pair of socks he had worn all week! That boy's feet do not smell great even after a bath, so you can imagine what they smelled like now. Going around all day breathing in that **stench** is torture!

And what's more, this pair has a hole worn in one of the socks. The hole sits over his **verruca**. With every step he takes, his **disgusting** verruca presses into my lovely face. Yuck!

I am <u>green with</u> **envy** when I look at Meg and Mel's shoes in a lovely, neat row. I watch as they carefully place them onto their feet.

Tom, <u>on the other hand</u>, doesn't even bother **untying** my laces to put me on. He just **crams** his foot down and wriggles it about until it's in. It hurts so much. It's <u>a hard knock life</u> for me!

Today was a no-uniform day at school for Tom. I thought the day was **improving** at first, but it was not to be.

Tom's teacher, Ms Carol, had moved his desk next to a rad. For a couple of hours, I was warm and cosy, tucked nicely under the desk. I was enjoying chatting to my friends, Doc Marten, Belinda Boot and Rachel Reebok.

"What a nice lady Tom's teacher is!" I thought at the time.

Boy, was I wrong... she is just like all of the other teachers!

"Looks like the rain has cleared, children," she said. "Let's get out in the fresh air."

"But it has been <u>raining cats and dogs</u> all week!" is what I was screaming out. No one was listening.

You know what a week of rain does to a football field? Muck, muck and more muck! Thick, oozy muck.

I hate yard breaks <u>at the best of times</u>. It's horrible out there on the football field. The screams of the other shoes as their owners smash them against the ball <u>sends shivers down</u> my sole. I spend every second hoping that the ball stays away from Tom. However, he always gets a kick.

Today was even worse. With every step Tom took, I got **caked** in mud. With every move, I was **squelched** down into it. But mud was <u>the least of my worries</u> today.

Lainey Lawrance's dog, who lives across the street, had followed her to school. When I looked down, there it was... a large, steaming pile of fresh brown poo!

I screamed, oh how I screamed, but Tom didn't hear me. He never does. I was helpless as he pressed me down into the big pile of poo. I was covered in the stuff and the smell was **disgusting**! You all know the smell of dog poo? Well, imagine having it smeared all over your face! Not a very nice thought, is it?

It's no joke being one of Tom's shoes, but every cloud has a silver lining. When his mam saw the state of me, she went crazy. After she had calmed down, she said it was time that he got a new pair. She's taking him to the shoe shop at the weekend.

Finally, I will be able to relax and enjoy my **retirement**.

I'm not sure what happens when you retire, but I think you go to a warm, cosy place that smells nice. I bet there's a large flat screen TV and relaxing music being played. Yes, that must be what happens to old shoes like me.

Anyway, I only have a few more days until I go to my new home. I can't wait!

A Closet Full of Shoes

by Shel Silverstein

Party shoes with frills and bows,
Workin' shoes with steel toes,
Sneakers, flip-flops, and galoshes,
Boots to wear with mackintoshes,
Brogans, oxfords, satin pumps,
Dancin' taps and wooden clumps,
Shoes for climbin', shoes for hikes,
Football cleats and baseball spikes,
Shoes of shiny patent leather,
Woolly shoes for winter weather,
Loafers, rough-outs, sandals, spats,
High heels, low heels, platforms, flats,
Moccasins and fins and flippers,
Shower clogs and ballet slippers...
A zillion shoes and just one missin'—
That's the one that matches this'n.

#STORMOPHELIA

6

My reading goal ★ Play with sounds in words such as syllables.

Here in Kerrypike National School, we have started something new and surprising. Homework has been banned!

Woah Nelly, <u>hold your horses</u>! Don't start a **jig** just yet!

Yes, homework as we know it has <u>vanished into thin air</u>. Of course, there is something else in its place (come on, don't be lazy), and yes, it is a *lot* cooler!

43

Our principal, Mrs Lynch says that we are <u>whizz kids</u> with **technology**, but we need to use our **devices** to learn things and not just to watch funny videos.

So, instead of homework, we now have home projects. These are much more interesting and less of a **chore**.

We get our project topic on Friday and we have a week to **complete** it. We know what you are thinking: homework at the weekend.

But you can decide for yourself when to do it. Plus, your family members can help out too!

When it's finished, we take turns to **present** it to the class. We also have a question-and-answer round, which is really fun. You should <u>give it a shot</u>.

Our home project this week was on Storm Ophelia. Have you heard anything about it?

We looked up websites, newspaper reports, images and videos about the storm.

The #who #what #where #when #why of Storm Ophelia

#stormophelia #thelowdown

On **Monday October 16th, 2017**, a storm began to brew in Ireland.

Firstly, a <u>status red weather warning</u> was put in place. This helped people to get ready for the bad weather.

Next, the wind began to grow. Soon, it **howled** and brought heavy rainfall. Storm Ophelia <u>smashed and bashed</u> the country as it went.

Meanwhile, there was a lot of travel **disruption**. There were no trains, buses or ferries, etc. The wind was too strong to travel in.

Then, schools and businesses were **forced** to close for <u>days on end</u>.

After that, the electricity went. Around 330,000 homes were without power.

No electricity meant no lights, TV, tablets or phones, unless people had **cordless charging**.

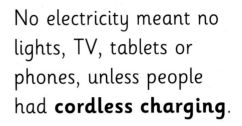

Once I got over the shock and had a good cry, I had lots of fun playing board games, doing art and building with Lego.

I didn't know what to do with myself on the first day. My fingers were **twitching**. I was swiping the glass in the windows at home, remembering what life was like with my good old friend the iPad.

<u>Not only that</u>, but many homes had no water either, because the pipes burst. That made toileting a big **issue**!

47

Sadly, three people died in the storm. One woman died after the car she was travelling in was **struck** by a falling tree in Waterford. A man was killed while clearing a fallen tree with a chainsaw in Tipperary. Another man died in Louth after a tree fell on his car. **#thejournal.ie**

In Cork, the roof of Cork City soccer club's **stadium** blew off, just one day before the team hoped to lift the League of Ireland trophy. **#times.com**

The storm caused lots and lots of damage. There were fallen trees, fallen branches, fallen electricity lines, bins blown over and shed roofs taken off.

Later, the storm was **upgraded** to a hurricane.

Finally, the storm eased off and life returned to normal.

We will never forget Storm Ophelia. It was the worst storm in Ireland for 50 years.

The Storm
by Jaymie Gerard

Before the storm
The sky turns grey
The clouds roll in
The sun tucks away

During the storm
The strong wind blows
The sky is wild
The rainwater flows

After the storm
The clouds say "adieu"
The sun peeks back out
The sky turns to blue

Pen Pals

Tom has a pen pal named Aarav, who lives in Mumbai in India. They met at a **culture** day in Tom's local café. **Lately**, they have been writing to tell each other about how they have been **preparing** for Christmas.

To: aaravlamba@schoolmail.com

Subject: Advent wreaths

Hi Aarav,

Hope <u>all is well</u> in Mumbai.

Yesterday, we made Advent wreaths at school. These are circles of wreath on **oasis**. There are five candles stuck into the oasis, three purple, one pink and one white.

First, my teacher, Ms Carol, set up four **station** tables. She put all of the oases at one station, the leaves at another, the candles at the third and decorations such as acorns, berries and baubles, at the last station.

Next, she made one herself, showing us all of the steps and where the different things go.

Then, she put on some Christmas songs while we worked. (My favourite is 'Merry Christmas Everyone'. Do you know it?) We took turns going around to the different stations to **assemble** our wreaths.

Finally, we had our wreaths blessed by the priest.

We will light a candle each Sunday in <u>the lead up</u> to Christmas and on Christmas Day we will light the white one.

What kinds of things do you do for Christmas?

Slán,

Tom

To: tomkelly@schoolmail.com

Subject: Star paper lanterns

Hi Tom,

The Advent wreath is really nice.

We made a Christmas item at school **on Thursday**. It was a paper **lantern** in the shape of a star. We will use them for our lantern festival on Christmas Eve. We hang the lanterns between our houses so that the stars float above us as we walk down the road.

First, our teacher, Mr Kumar, gave us the **template** of the star.

Next, we cut, folded and glued it so that it became a 3-D star shape.

After that, we **sewed** all of the edges together using a needle and thread.

Finally, we decorated our star lanterns using different colours and patterns.

What do you eat in Ireland at Christmas time?

Namaste,

Aarav

To: aaravlamba@schoolmail.com

Subject: Christmas dinner in Ireland

Dia dhuit Aarav,

The paper lantern festival sounds really cool!

Now that I am thinking about food, my <u>tummy is rumbling</u>!

Every Christmas we have the same thing and it is so tasty!

First, we have a starter – usually melon or vegetable soup.

Then, it's the main course – turkey, ham, stuffing, mashed potato, roast potato, potato **croquettes**, carrots, Brussels sprouts and gravy. A lot of potatoes, right?

After that, it's onto dessert. Mam usually has three different **types** – Christmas cake with brandy sauce for my nana and grandad, mince pies with cream for my dad and Uncle Seán and jelly and ice cream for all the kids.

Finally, in the evening, we eat the leftover turkey and ham in sandwiches and some chocolate from our **selection** boxes.

How about you? What do you eat in Mumbai at Christmas time?

Slán,

Tom

To: tomkelly@schoolmail.com

Subject: Christmas food in Mumbai

Namaste Tom,

Wow that is a lot of food! It sounds tasty.

Last year, we had lots of sweet treats.

To begin with, we took part in *consuada*, which is when we make sweets for our family and friends for Christmas.

Then, we got to eat all of the things we had made!

First, we had a **traditional** rich fruit cake.

Then, we had lots of sweets like *neureos*, which are small fried **pastries** stuffed with dried fruit and coconut.

After that, we had *dodol*, which is a type of toffee with coconut and cashew.

Finally, we had **marzipan** fruit shapes.

I could not <u>move a muscle</u> after all of that, so I lay on the sofa playing with my toys.

Do you have Christmas trees and Santa Claus in Ireland? We decorate banana or mango trees for *Bada Din*. (That is what we call Christmas. It means 'Big Day'.) Santa delivers presents by horse and cart here and the weather is usually hot.

Alavida,

Aarav

Subject: The Panto and The Toy Show

Hey Aarav,

I had a really busy day today.

First, I went to the panto. Our entire school went. It was a show on stage in a big **theatre** in the city. It was 'Jack and the Beanstalk' this year. We really enjoyed it.

Then, I wrote my letter to Santa. This year I am asking Santa for a bike and a surprise.

After that, we went to a carol concert in the local **community** hall. We all sang Christmas carols and the lights on the big Christmas tree were switched on. We had hot chocolate and mince pies too.

Finally, we watched the *Late Late Toy Show* (that is why I am emailing so late). This is a big Irish tradition. The most **popular** toys of the year are shown by children from <u>across the nation</u>. My family and I all sat down together to watch it. Meg fell asleep.

To answer your questions about Santa and Christmas trees: yes, we have both too! The trees that we decorate are fir, **spruce** or pine and Santa delivers his presents on a sleigh.

<u>I must dash</u> now. I will email you again soon.

Chat later,

Tom

P.S. It is almost always cold here and we get lots and lots of rain!

How to Make a Friend
by Jane Heitman Healy

You start by saying *Hi there,*
Hello, Aloha, Ciao –
If someone answers back to you,
Smile and nod and bow.

You might try saying *Hola,*
Salut, Goddag, Shalom.
If someone answers back to you,
They might be far from home.

A friend begins by greeting
Those they meet along the way
To make them feel welcome
At home, at school, at play.

A Merry Messi Christmas Play

8

My reading goal ★ Improve the pace of my reading.

THE CAST

NARRATOR 1

NARRATOR 2

EVAN

ELLA

SANTA

MRS CLAUS

MESSI

ELF KEVIN

ELF INSPECTOR 1

ELF INSPECTOR 2

OTHER ELVES 1–6

Scene 1

Evan, Ella and Baby Ed's House

Narrator 1: It was the night before Christmas, and all through the Mooney house, not a creature was **stirring** not even a mouse.

Narrator 2: Well actually, that's not quite true. There was a little elf crying.

Elf Kevin: Boo hoo, hoo hoo.

(Ella and Evan don't hear him.)

Elf Kevin: *(louder)* BOO HOO, HOO HOO!

(Ella and Evan still don't hear him.)

Elf Kevin: COME 'ERE, GIRL! I'M <u>CRYIN' MY EYES OUT</u> OVER HERE!

Ella: Oh my, who are you and what is the matter? I thought it was Baby Ed making that **clatter**.

Narrator 1: He seemed to be shaking, as he started to chatter.

Elf Kevin: My name is Elf Kevin. I'm from the North Pole. I'm going to be sick. Please pass me a bowl!

Narrator 1: The elf explained the problem at hand. The North Pole finally got Sky this year and **fibre broadband**!

Narrator 2: But now our dear Santa is **addicted** to Sky. He won't get out of his chair. He won't let the reindeer fly.

Narrator 1: He said he's not going to deliver the presents this year. He has <u>lost the plot</u>! We're in **utter despair**!

Evan: That's terrible. What about my Xbox?

Elf Kevin: You won't even be getting a cereal box <u>at this rate</u>. I think we will have to cancel Christmas!

(Everyone gasps.)

Narrator 1: Evan then offered to help if he can. He wasn't sure what to do, but the elf had a plan.

Narrator 2: He would take them to the North Pole to get Santa out of his **rut**. It's time the big fella got up off his…

Narrator 1: *(shouts)* Chair!

Elf Kevin: Time for some fairy dust. ♫

(Elf Kevin, Evan and Ella leave the stage.)

Scene 2
The North Pole

(Evan, Ella and Elf Kevin fly past.)

Narrator 1: Evan, Ella and Elf Kevin finally reached the North Pole.

Narrator 2: Where penguins were dancing from igloo to hole.

Elf Kevin: Come on, Santa's workshop is just up ahead. Be careful not to **damage** the sled.

(At the North Pole, the whole class are penguins and do the penguin dance. 🎵)

Scene 3
Santa's workshop

Narrator 1: At **headquarters**, the Elf Inspectors are checking toys and going **berserk**. All the poor elves are tired from their hard work. 🎵

Elf Inspector 1: Right, how is the yo-yo department doing?

Elf 1: A bit up and down, but we're getting there.

*(Elf 2 is **rapping** to himself.)*

Elf Inspector 1: What are you doing?

Elf 2: You told me to get **wrapping** earlier, so I am.

(Elf 3 runs in with a sack of rubber ducks.)

Elf 3: Here they are, sir, just like you asked – a thousand Christmas quackers.

Elf Inspector 2: Christmas crackers, you silly elf, not quackers!

(Elf 3 runs off crying.)

Elf 4: You shouldn't shout at her.

Elf 5: Yeah, she already has low elf-esteem.

Elf Inspector 2: So, will the presents be ready?

Elf 6: What's the point in having the presents ready? The big guy is still watching sport. He won't deliver any.

Scene 4

Santa's house

Narrator 1: Santa's watching the match. There's a new player on the team. Her name's Cinderella. She's more nightmare than dream.

Santa: Cinderella, you're useless! My nan would have scored that!

Mrs Claus: Calm down, dear, it's only a game. Keep on your hat!

Narrator 1: Cinderella is bad at soccer. She always runs from the ball. And she only wears one boot, so no wonder she falls.

Narrator 2: And her coach is a pumpkin. She should go back to soccer school.

Narrator 1: But she's still better than anyone at Liverpool!

Everyone: OOOOOOOOOOOOOOOOOOOOHHHHHHH!

Elf Kevin: Sir, I've brought someone to talk to you.

Santa: Can't you see I'm busy?

Elf Kevin: But it's important.

Santa: OK, what is it?

Ella: It's about Christmas. I heard you aren't delivering the presents this year.

Santa: That's right. I'm <u>fed up with it</u> and there's a big match on tonight. I'm not missing that, so I'm not taking flight. I've a plateful of cookies and a jugful of milk. I feel so relaxed and <u>my skin feels like silk</u>.

(Evan and Ella take Elf Kevin over to the side and whisper in his ear.)

Ella: I have an idea.

Narrator 1: Ella explains to Elf Kevin that she has an idea. She knows where Messi's holiday home is. Just let her on Google and she is a whizz.

Narrator 2: It's down by her nan's house. It's really not far and easy to find, if you follow the North Star.

(Elf Kevin, Evan and Ella go and bring back Messi.)

Messi: Hey there, big guy. What's all this about cancelling Christmas?

Santa: Wow, Messi! What brings you to this **patch**? Sure I can't deliver the presents, I want to watch your match!

Messi: You can't cancel Christmas. It's too important, you see. You were the one who gave me my first football at the age of three. Anyway, why not **record** it? Have you never heard of Sky Q? it's the new ultra HD box that records ten channels at once for you.

(Messi gives him a Sky Q box.)

Santa: OK, Messi, I'll do it, anything for you. But could you then make the score of the match 2:2?

(Santa gives him a wink. ♫)

Santa: OK, let's go. To the reindeer!

Scene 5

The Stable

Narrator 1: However, there was another problem at the stable. Rudolph had been eating too many cakes, so he just wasn't able...

Narrator 2: ...to help pull the sleigh. He just cannot fly it. That reindeer, he needed to go on a **diet**. ♫

Narrator 1: So the reindeer were **prepped** and the sleigh was made ready. The sack was full of toys. Indeed, it was heavy.

Narrator 2: After all the drama, Santa was at last ready to go, and all that he needed was a...

Santa: Ho, ho, ho!

All: Merry Christmas, everyone!

(Santa gets pulled out the door in his sleigh. ♫)

The Blizzard of 1947

9

My reading goal ★ Listen to a report and give my opinion.

<u>You won't believe your ears</u> when you hear our news! Ella and I have won a competition and are going to Met Éireann Headquarters in Dublin. We will **present** a report from the studio there.

When Ms Carol told us about the competition, we had <u>ants in our pants</u>. When we were paired up together, we <u>jumped for joy</u>. After all, Ella and I were like <u>two peas in a pod</u> and now we were going to be famous!

We spent <u>morning, noon and night</u> preparing. We were **eager** to win.

We began to gather information, choose what was important, then **draft**, edit and redraft our work.

We hope you will find it as interesting as we do!

Tom and Ella Reporting on the Blizzard of 1947

This morning we would like you to <u>cast your minds back</u> to 1947 to tell you all about the blizzard that happened that year.

A blizzard is a snowstorm that can last a long time. It brings very strong wind and lots of snowfall. The wind can be as powerful as a hurricane. (Do you remember Storm Ophelia?)

The blizzard of 1947 is described by weather forecasters as "the coldest and harshest winter in living memory." We say 'winter', but, the wintry weather of that year began in February and lasted through to May!

On February 24th, after a **mild** winter, snow began to fall in Ireland. This was the start of an Arctic snowstorm!

At first, people smiled as they watched the <u>blanket of snow</u> **transform** the place. They imagined snowball fights, snowmen building, and, if they were lucky enough, a day or two off school.

However, what was to follow soon <u>wiped the smiles clean off their faces</u>. The snow, which was <u>mounting by the minute</u>, was there to stay. It lingered and lingered for 50 days!

The country was pounded from <u>head to toe</u> by a powerful blizzard. For the next few months, temperatures **rarely** rose above freezing point. The people of Ireland were not ready for it.

At that time, Ireland had only a few weather forecasters and there was no TV. There was no internet either, so people couldn't check the weather <u>at the touch of a button</u> like they can nowadays.

Postmen became like weather **prophets**. They gave the locals their weather predictions as they tried to make their way <u>from pillar to post</u>.

Many people were left **isolated** <u>for weeks on end</u>. Some folk even got lost in the blizzard as they bravely left their homes in search of food and fuel.

With nothing to heat their homes, some people had to burn their furniture just to get a bit of heat.

The heavy snowfall made all road and rail travel <u>ground to a halt</u>. Shops were without fresh food. Hospitals were without supplies. Many animals and crops **perished**.

With people in low spirits, the locals from Lough Key tried to make the best of a bad situation. Many of the families who lived around the lake were great dancers. They danced a *céilí* on the frozen lake and spent some great evenings together on the ice.

Sadly, at least 600 people died in Ireland that year because of the harsh cold.

And who knows when a weather event like this will hit the country again? The question is, will the Irish **nation** be ready?

You've been listening to Ella and Tom. Over and out.

Presenter: Thank you, Tom and Ella. That was **fascinating**. What inspired you to write this report?

Tom: It was this photograph.

Presenter: Can you explain it to our listeners, please?

Tom: This was taken during Storm Emma, also known as the 'Beast from the East'. Storm Emma was a very heavy blizzard that happened in Ireland on March 1st, 2018.

Ella: We had no school for three days! Tom and I are next-door neighbours, so we spent some time on the net, researching blizzards in Ireland. When we **discovered** the blizzard of 1947, we knew it would be great for this competition.

Presenter: That's amazing. Well done and thank you for coming in today. Your teacher will be very proud. You have been listening to School FM. We'll be back after a short break.

Snow Day
by Barbara Vance

In the winter, it's every kid's dream,
As snowflakes begin to appear,
That suddenly there'll be a blizzard,
And they'll cancel school for the year.

Though most kids are willing to settle,
And I am inclined to agree,
They could merely close school for one day –
One day off would be just fine with me.

A day free from all forms of homework,
A day without science or math,
When you leave all your school books at home –
And run out the door with a laugh.

A day full of sledding and cocoa
And snowmen who wear Dad's old clothes;
No writing out boring equations
After lunch when you'd rather just doze.

A snow day's a day meant for lounging,
Where idleness isn't condemned,
A day where you sleep in till lunchtime,
A day that you don't want to end.

And if you are truly quite lucky,
The snow will continue its flight,
And you'll spend the afternoon hoping
The next day will be just as white.

Tom Goes to China

10

My reading goal ★ Read and talk about the interesting parts of this text.

Tom, Meg and Mel <u>set off</u> on a trip to China **recently**. Dad was working there for a few weeks. The family were <u>thrilled to pieces</u> when they got to go with him.

China is a large country in Asia. It is the fourth largest country in the world. The **capital** city is Beijing and the main language spoken there is Mandarin.

Tom got a **brochure** about some of the different things that happen in China. Let's <u>take a closer look</u>.

Chinese New Year

The date on which Chinese New Year falls changes every year. This is because in China, they follow the **lunar** calendar. The word 'lunar' means moon. The moon **completes** its journey around the Earth every 29½ days. Chinese New Year falls on a day between mid-January and mid-February. Their New Year Festival lasts for 15 days.

Chinese New Year parade

In China, each year is **represented** by one of 12 animals. These are the dragon, the snake, the horse, the goat (or sheep), the monkey, the rooster, the dog, the pig, the rat, the ox, the tiger and the rabbit. The Chinese believe that the animal matching the year in which you were born can tell you a lot about your **personality** and your future. According to an old saying, "This animal hides in your heart."

YEAR OF THE	DATES ON WHICH NEW YEAR FALLS			
dragon	**2000** February 5	**2012** January 23	**2024** February 10	**2036** January 28
snake	**2001** January 4	**2013** February 10	**2025** January 29	**2037** February 15
horse	**2002** February 12	**2014** January 31	**2026** February 17	**2038** February 4
goat	**2003** February 1	**2015** February 19	**2027** February 6	**2039** January 24
monkey	**2004** January 22	**2016** February 8	**2028** January 26	**2040** February 12
rooster	**2005** February 9	**2017** January 28	**2029** February 13	**2041** February 1
dog	**2006** January 29	**2018** February 16	**2030** February 3	**2042** January 22
pig	**2007** February 18	**2019** February 5	**2031** January 23	**2043** February 10
rat	**2008** February 7	**2020** January 25	**2032** February 11	**2044** January 30
ox	**2009** January 26	**2021** February 12	**2033** January 31	**2045** February 17
tiger	**2010** February 14	**2022** February 1	**2034** February 19	**2046** February 6
rabbit	**2011** February 3	**2023** January 22	**2035** February 8	**2047** January 26

Chinese Lantern Festival

Lighting a paper lantern

The Chinese Lantern Festival can be <u>traced back</u> to 2,000 years ago. This festival **marks** the end of the Chinese New Year Festival.

Billions of paper lanterns are lit during the Lantern Festival. People go outside at night-time to look at the moon. They send up flying lanterns and fly bright **drones**. They have a meal and enjoy time together with family and friends.

Lighting lanterns is a way for people to pray that they will have a **smooth** future and **express** their best wishes for their family.

Releasing paper lanterns

The artwork on some lanterns shows **traditional** Chinese images and symbols such as fruit, flowers, birds, animals, people and buildings.

Lantern-owners stick riddles on the lanterns. People crowd round to guess the riddles. If someone thinks they have the right answer, they can pull the riddle off and go to the lantern-owner to check their answer. If the answer is right, there is usually a small gift as a prize.

After the Lantern Festival, all of the New Year decorations are taken down. This marks the start of spring.

The Dragon Boat Festival

1. A public holiday

The Dragon Boat Festival is an important public holiday in China. People have the day off. It is like Saint Patrick's Day in Ireland. Dragon Boat Racing takes place during this festival.

2. The festival date changes

The date of the festival changes each year. It takes place on the fifth day of the fifth month **according** to the lunar calendar. This day falls between May 25th and July 24th.

3. In memory of a Chinese poet

The Dragon Boat Festival remembers the poet Qu Yuan, who died over 2,000 years ago. It is said that he drowned in the Miluo River on the fifth day of the fifth lunar month.

Dragon Boat Racing

4. Dragon Boat Racing

When Qu Yuan drowned, the local people raced their boats to search for him. They dropped lumps of rice into the water so that the fish would not <u>feast on</u> his body. <u>In order to</u> remember Qu Yuan, this **practice** continues today with Dragon Boat Racing.

5. Eating *zongzi* is the most popular custom

On the morning of the Dragon Boat Festival, every family eats *zongzi*. These are rice **dumplings** wrapped in **bamboo** leaves. They are made of sticky rice stuffed with different fillings. People usually prepare them the day before the festival.

Grandma's zongzi are yum!

Especially with spicy dip

6. Special plants are hung on doors

People hang Chinese **mugwort** and **calamus** on their doors for the Dragon Boat Festival. These are herbs. They do this <u>in the belief</u> that the herbs <u>drive away</u> evil and diseases. They are also believed to bring good luck.

Oh, the Places You'll Go
by Dr Seuss

Congratulations!
Today is your day.
You're off to Great Places!
You're off and away!
You have brains in your head.
You have feet in your shoes.
You can steer yourself
any direction you choose.
You're on your own. And you know what you know.
And YOU are the guy who'll decide where to go.
You'll look up and down streets. Look 'em over with care.
About some you will say, "I don't choose to go there."
With your head full of brains and your shoes full of feet,
you're too smart to go down any not-so-good street.
And you may not find any
you'll want to go down.
In that case, of course,
you'll head straight out of town.
It's opener there
in the wide open air.
Out there things can happen
and frequently do
to people as brainy
and footsy as you.
And then things start to happen,
don't worry. Don't stew.
Just go right along.
You'll start happening too.
OH! THE PLACES YOU'LL GO!

Spring Feasts

Tom and Ella's latest home project is about spring feasts. On Grandparents' Day last week, many of the nanas and grandads helped them with their project. Here is what they found out.

Saint Bridget's Day

Saint Bridget was born in County Louth in the year 453 AD. <u>From a very early age</u>, she was known for her kindness. When she was a young girl, she heard Saint Patrick **preaching** and became interested in prayer.

Bridget decided that she wanted to live a life of prayer and help poor people. She was sent to a bishop in Longford, who set up a house for her and some other girls. They became the first nuns in Ireland.

There are many stories about Saint Bridget that may only be **legends**. **Nevertheless**, they are good tales. One tale tells us that she and her sisters once went on a long journey and <u>came across</u> the castle of a local king. The king was away hunting, but his sons welcomed them and gave them food.

Bridget **noticed** harps hanging on the walls. She asked the young men to play some music. They told her that they were unable to play and that the harpists were away with their father, the king.

Bridget told them to hold out their hands. She touched their fingers with her own and then told them to play. <u>To everyone's amazement</u>, they played music more beautiful than anyone had ever heard.

When Bridget died, her body was brought to Downpatrick in Ulster and buried beside Saint Patrick's grave. She is remembered for her **holiness** on February 1st. People make special crosses woven out of **rushes** on this day. They hang them over doorways and windows to protect their homes from any kind of harm.

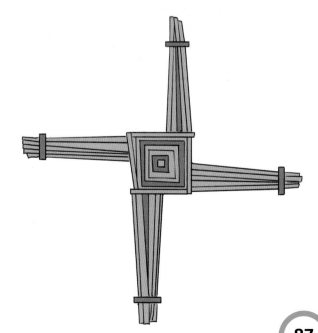

Shrove Tuesday

Shrove Tuesday marks the beginning of Lent. During the six weeks of Lent, many people give up **luxuries** such as sweets and toys. Long ago, Shrove Tuesday was seen as a chance to use up 'luxury' foods such as butter and eggs before Lent began. This is why pancakes are still eaten on this day.

Shrove Tuesday takes place 47 days before Easter Sunday and falls between February 3rd and March 9th. It is **celebrated** all over the world, but is known by different names.

In Ireland, Britain and Australia, it is known as Pancake Day or Pancake Tuesday. In France, they **refer** to it as *Mardi Gras*, meaning 'fat Tuesday'. In Iceland, they celebrate *Sprengidagur*, which means 'the day of bursting'. In Greece, it is called *Apocreas*, meaning 'of the meat', as this is the last time many people eat meat before Easter Sunday.

Saint Valentine's Day

Saint Valentine was a third-century Roman saint. He was born in the year 226 AD. Not much is known about his life, but it is **agreed** that he was **martyred**. To be martyred means to be killed because of your beliefs.

According to one story, while Saint Valentine was a bishop, a judge named Asterius put him under **house arrest**. They talked about religion and Asterius decided to put Valentine's faith <u>to the test</u>.

Asterius presented his blind daughter to Valentine and told him to **restore** (bring back) her sight. Valentine placed his hands over the child's eyes and she began to see again!

Saint Valentine's Day is celebrated all over the world on February 14th. It is a day **associated** with love. People send cards, give presents and write poems to their loved ones.

Saint Patrick's Day

Saint Patrick is the **patron** saint of Ireland. A patron saint is the saint who protects a person or place. Patrick was born in the year 385 AD in Britain.

Britain is the land that is next to Ireland. England, Scotland and Wales are countries in Britain.

When Patrick was 16 years old, Irish raiders attacked his family's **estate**. They **captured** Patrick and took him to Ireland. He was <u>held captive</u> for nearly six years and lived a lonely life as a shepherd.

From Patrick's writings, we know that he believed God came to him in a dream and told him to leave Ireland. He **escaped** and walked over 300 kilometres before he found a ship to take him home to Britain.

After 15 years of study, Patrick was **ordained** a priest and sent back to Ireland to tell the people about God. He used the shamrock and explained that its three leaves were like the Father, the Son and the Holy Spirit.

He is also famous for <u>driving all of the snakes into the sea</u>, so that to this day, there are no snakes lurking in the beautiful green grass of Ireland. We celebrate Saint Patrick's Day on March 17th.

It's the Wearing of the Green Day
by Brenda Williams

It's the wearing of the green day
The wearing of the green!
For all around this Emerald Isle
The shamrock can be seen!
It's the wearing of the green day
The day we celebrate
St Patrick and his message
On this most important date.
It's the wearing of the green day
In this land of hills and lakes
Where St Patrick had the wisdom
To banish all the snakes.
It's the wearing of the green day
A time to dance and sing
For the sound of Irish music
Brings a welcome touch of spring.
It's the wearing of the green day
When we remember well
The Shamrock and its three leaves
And the story they can tell.
It's the wearing of the green day
So follow the parades
We'll beat the drums and play the pipes
Until the daylight fades.

Superman, my Superhero

My reading goal ★ Think about why the author wrote this text.

Ella and Tom have been doing home projects about their favourite superheroes. Ms Carol said they could pick any person they liked. They had to do some **research** to find information about their superhero.

Here is a <u>sneak peek</u> at Tom's project. His superhero is Superman. He will tell you about an actor who played Superman in the movies.

The character of Superman was created by Jerry Siegel and Joe Shuster in 1933 and was published by DC Comics.

Who Is Superman?

<u>First things first</u>, who is Superman and what does he do? Superman is a **being** from another planet. He is the only **survivor** of the planet Krypton.

Jonathan and Martha Kent found him inside a **vessel** as a baby and brought him to their farm in Smallville. To them, he looked human. The Kents named the baby Clark and raised him as their own son.

As Clark grew older, he found out he had superpowers. He wanted to use his powers to help others. He helped people in danger and stopped bad things from happening. He got a job as a **reporter** for the *Daily Planet* after he wrote a story about Superman.

Superman has **tremendous** strength and he can fly! His sharp senses allow him to hear sounds that are so quiet, they cannot be heard by human beings.

Your five senses are sight, hearing, touch, taste and smell.

His 'zoom **vision**' allows him to see things that are far away. His 'X-ray vision' allows him to see through **solid** objects such as walls. He also has the power to make heat within objects, which is known as 'heat vision'.

Kryptonite, a rock from the planet on which he was born, could kill Superman within minutes, **especially** if it fell into the wrong hands. Lex Luthor is Superman's **enemy** and tries to destroy him.

Christopher Reeve

Christopher Reeve was born on September 25th, 1952 in New York City. He was a **talented** actor. He became famous for his **role** as the comic-book superhero, Superman. He was also a very active man and enjoyed horse riding.

However, Christopher had an accident that changed his life. Shortly before this accident, he played the role of a **paralysed** policeman in a film. He did research at a **rehabilitation** (re-hab-il-it-a-tion) centre. This is a special hospital, where people go to recover from an accident. He learned how to use a wheelchair to get in and out of a car.

On May 27th, 1995, he was taking part in a horse-riding competition. **Witnesses** said that his horse began its third fence jump and suddenly stopped.

Christopher fell forward off the horse, while still holding onto the **reins**. His hands became **tangled** in the reins and he landed headfirst on the other side of the fence.

His neck was broken and he was left paralysed. For the first few days after the accident, he was in shock. He woke up **confused**, saying things like "get the gun" and "they're after us". He became a wheelchair user. He also needed a machine called a **ventilator** to help him to breathe.

A doctor tried to fix Christopher's neck by fitting a piece of bone from his hip into his **spinal column**.

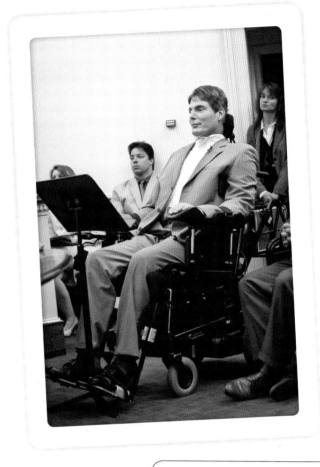

This is your spinal column. Try to feel it with your fingers.

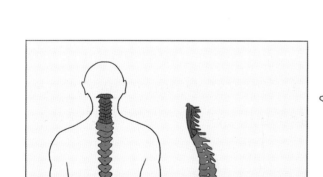

On June 28th, 1995, Christopher was taken to a rehabilitation centre. It reminded him of the centre he had been to when he played the role of the policeman in a wheelchair a few years earlier.

He was <u>over the moon</u> when he began to move the **index** finger of his left hand. Later, he was able to move his arms and legs <u>ever so slightly</u>. His breathing tube fell out many times and the nurses had to rush in to save his life.

It was <u>a long road</u> and he knew that he would never walk again, but he tried to stay **positive**. He decided to use his fame to help people with spinal injuries. He set up the Christopher Reeve Foundation.

Index finger

Paralympic athletes

Christopher's **disability** did not stop him from doing what he loved. He continued to act and make movies. He also hosted the Paralympics in Atlanta.

Christopher wrote a book about his life. In the book, he described his accident, saying, "and then I left my body. I was up on the ceiling... I looked down and saw my body stretched out on the bed, not moving. The noise... grew quieter as though someone were gradually turning down the volume."

He used special exercise machines to keep his muscles strong. He wanted his body to be strong enough in case a **cure** was ever found.

A book about your life that you wrote yourself is called an autobiography.

In October 2004, Christopher had an **ulcer** that became infected. On October 9th, he felt fine and went to his son Will's hockey match. That night, he went into **cardiac arrest**. He fell into a **coma** and died the next day, aged 52.

If I Could Be A Super Hero
by Steve Lazarowitz

I don't think I could be Superman

I'm sort of scared of heights

I'd sort of like to be Spiderman

But I'm afraid of spider bites

I suppose I could be Wolverine

But I'm afraid people would stare

I'd consider being The Incredible Hulk

But radiation's bad for your hair

Captain America, him perhaps

I love his mighty shield

But I fear I'm not brave enough

When things get rough, I yield

If I could be a superhero

I wonder which I'd be

Or maybe it's time I tried to find

The hero inside of me.

The Witch's Lair

Did you hear the news about the scouts who got lost when they went camping? Evan and I were there! We were **supposed** to tent up near the Ailwee Caves, but a thick yellow fog set in. The scout leaders found a new spot that wasn't too far away. Once the tents had gone up, they went to set up some outdoor lights.

"Don't move a muscle while we're gone," they **warned**.

But we did not listen. We went for a stroll, got lost and ended up in a deep, dark **lair**. It seemed to swallow us up, because in no time at all, we were faced with our worst nightmare. It was a witch's lair!

Evan had his phone. There was no **reception**, but the torch for the camera was a big help. Here's what we saw:

101

HOW TO TURN A CHILD INTO A FROG

WHAT DO I NEED?

1 disgusting child

1 cup of fairy wings

2 cups of slug slime

3 spoonfuls of unicorn tears

2 crunchy toenails

WHAT MUST I DO?

Step 1: Gather the ingredients and drop them into a **cauldron** of boiling milk.

Step 2: Stir them around five times using <u>the tail end</u> of a witch's broom.

Step 3: Take the child out of its cage.

Step 4: Say the following words while looking at the child: Eye of **newt** and ear of **hog**, turn this child into a frog!

Step 5: Place the frog into a frog jar.

Warning: May need to be repeated if the child starts growing back inside jar.

HOW TO PUT SOMEONE TO SLEEP FOR A CENTURY

WHAT DO I NEED?

1 toadstool

2 dragon scales

1 cup of cat pee

5 thorns from a blackberry bush

3 drops of fresh blood

WHAT MUST I DO?

Step 1: Chop the dragon scales into **quarters** and place into a cauldron of boiling toadstool.

Step 2: Add the cat pee, stirring as you go.

Step 3: Sprinkle in the thorns, making sure to **prick** your finger on the last one.

Step 4: Squeeze in three drops of blood from the fresh cut.

Step 5: Stir and say the following **chant**: Bubble bubble alacareep, drink this potion and then you will sleep!

Tip: Add in a loud **cackle** for an even deeper sleep.

HOW TO MAKE
YOURSELF LOOK YOUNGER

WHAT DO I NEED?

Contents of one baby's nappy

The **dew** of 3 daffodils

2 bottles of children's laughter
(horrible stuff)

The hairbrush of a Second Class girl

WHAT MUST I DO?

Step 1: Smear the contents of the baby's nappy onto your face. Leave for 20 minutes.

Step 2: Dab the dew from the daffodils under your eyes and onto your forehead.

Step 3: Breathe in the bottles of children's laughter.

Step 4: Comb your hair with the Second Class girl's hairbrush.

You should see **immediate** results. Repeat once a month.

Here is what we did: WE RAN!!!

We ran as fast <u>as our legs could carry us</u>!

Step 1: Back through the lair – tiptoe, tiptoe

Step 2: Back through the forest – stumble, trip, stumble trip

Step 3: Back around the lake – splash, splosh, splash splosh

Step 4: Back past the owl – hoot, hoot, hoot, hoot

Step 5: Back to the camp base – inhale, exhale, inhale, exhale

Step 6: Into our sleeping bags, zip them up, shiver and **shudder**, lie there **petrified**.

We are never going for a stroll in the dark again!

Witches' Delight
by Christy Ann Martine

I have a recipe
for witches' delight.
It's enough to make you
Want to take flight.

First, you add three
rattlesnake tails,
one cup curdled milk,
and a handful of snails.

Mix in a bucket,
stir with a mop,
then boil for one hour,
until slimy slop.

Sprinkle with bugs,
leave overnight,
and in the morning
you'll have quite a fright.

For there's nothing as
ghastly as witches' delight.

The 'How-to' Guide to Being Eight

My reading goal ★ Self-correct as I read: Does it look right, sound right and make sense?

It's tough being a kid. Sure, adults say that it's the best time of your life, but they've forgotten about the bad bits.

Wearing school uniforms, having to do what you're told and eat all of your vegetables before you can have dessert... it's <u>no walk in the park</u>.

I'm sure you've tried to make life a little easier for yourself by taking a **shortcut** here and there.

There's no **shame** in that. You're young. You're still learning.

However, having been through it myself, I am going to share some tips that might help you survive being an eight-year-old.

How to Dodge Homework

Most kids do not like homework. It doesn't make sense. Adults don't do it. It's not as if a builder comes home from work and has to build a small wall in the front garden. It's ridiculous!

There is no way of getting off homework *every* night (unless you break your writing arm on purpose, which is a bit **extreme**!). However, you might be able to get away with it for one night.

Step 1: Make up a good excuse. Never say your dog ate it. This is the oldest trick in the book and teachers see straight through it. If your dog really did eat your homework, no one would believe you!

The more serious your excuse, the more your teacher will understand why your homework hasn't been done.

If your brother's head **exploded** at the dinner table, you wouldn't have to mop up his brains and then whip out your maths. However, the downside to an extreme lie is that it is less likely to be believed.

A **fib** like "all my pencils broke and I had no parer" might be better, but then your teacher might not **deem** it a good enough reason for not doing your homework.

Step 2: Consider your teacher… some teachers are smart, some are kind, others are just plain crazy! Remember this when **concocting** your fib.

Step 3: Tell the fib and stick to it no matter what! Teachers will ask **dozens** of questions to try and **expose** your fib, but if you stick to your story, there is really nothing they can do.

How to Get Off School

Sometimes you might not want to go to school. You might have a maths test, or maybe the principal is coming to **inspect** the school bags (you haven't cleaned out yours and there are bits of old food in it). You might just want to play on your games console all day. However, if you aren't sick, then you just have to go to school, right? Wrong!

Step 1: Start acting weird the night before. Try to look tired and give your tummy a bit of a rub every time you see your parents.

Step 2: The next morning, get hot. Do sit-ups and put a warm **flannel** on your head. Then, very quickly tell one of your parents that you are burning up. If you are fast enough, your temperature will still be high when the thermometer comes out.

Step 3: Make it sound worse than it is. Use things you have learned in drama class like throwing a hand up to your head or talking in a **hoarse** voice. This step will really help to seal the deal.

You could say that you have a sore throat, which comes with the added bonus of also getting ice cream.

Another option is to put something that looks like sick (soup or diced carrot) down the toilet. You should get the day off, but you would get no food all day and might be starving.

Step 4: Get your mam's lipstick and put dots all over your face. Plus: You will definitely get a day off. Minus: You will probably be marched straight to the doctor, who won't be as easily fooled as your mam.

How to Get the Toy You Want

It's not fair that kids have to save up for something they want. If an adult wants something (like petrol or **insurance**), they can get it **instantly** by using their credit card. Grown-ups don't know how lucky they are!

Step 1: Find the ideal toy. Don't rush your decision. Parents would prefer to spend hours walking around a toyshop than have you choose too quickly and **regret** your decision.

Step 2: Save! In the olden days, kids were allowed to work, the lucky ducks! Nowadays, we can't, but we can do **chores** around the house to earn a few extra euro.

Step 3: Another option is your teeth, which are little nuggets of gold. Imagine how much money you could get if you pulled them all out at once. They are going to come out **eventually** anyway! You could also try to **con** the Tooth Fairy. You might find a tiny stone that looks like a tooth and put it under your pillow. It's worth a shot!

I hope you have found this guide useful. But maybe this has left you wondering if it would be easier to do your homework or face the day in school rather than going through all the effort of trying not to. The choice is yours.

Homework! Oh, Homework!

by Jack Prelutsky

Homework! Oh, homework!
I hate you! You stink!
I wish I could wash you away in the sink,
if only a bomb
would explode you to bits.
Homework! Oh, homework!
You're giving me fits.

I'd rather take baths
with a man-eating shark,
or wrestle a lion
alone in the dark,
eat spinach and liver,
pet ten porcupines,
than tackle the homework,
my teacher assigns.

Homework! Oh, homework!
you're last on my list,
I simply can't see
why you even exist,
if you just disappeared
it would tickle me pink.
Homework! Oh, homework!
I hate you! You stink!

114

Lainey's Box of Delights

My reading goal ★ Choose and read a text for pleasure.

As you know, I'm Lainey and I am a Second Class pupil in Kerrypike National School. What you may not know about me is that I want to be Ireland's next Junior Masterchef!

You may have seen the show on TV. You need to be at least 10 years old to **apply**. So, I've got two years to wait.

"A long time away," you might think. "You'll have forgotten about it by then," you might say.

You're wrong. I've got a plan you see, a Masterchef masterplan!

Since the age of four, I have wanted to be a chef. Nana Smith **inspired** me. The smell of her queen cakes, the taste of her shepherd's pie, the flavour of her smoothies... mmm! She has taught me everything she knows.

Nana Smith has a very special recipe book. She calls it a family **heirloom**. It was given to her by her father, who was a chef in the army, and now she has passed it down to me.

Today is your lucky day. I'm going to show you the recipes I have been working on. I'd love to hear your feedback.

Egg and Soldiers

What do I need?

Ingredients	Utensils	
1 egg 7 asparagus spears	saucepans scoop plate	egg cup water knife

What do I do? (method)

Step 1: In a saucepan of boiling salted water, add the asparagus and cook until soft (**approximately** 10 minutes).

Step 2: In another saucepan, boil water and carefully drop in an egg. Keep it on the heat for approximately seven minutes.

Step 3: Carefully scoop the egg out of the water and place it in an egg cup. Cut the top off the soft-boiled egg.

Step 4: Serve with the asparagus for dipping.

Incredible Edible Facts

You can 'peel' hard-boiled eggs by blowing the egg right out of the shell. The word 'yolk' comes from an old English word that means 'yellow'.

Frozen Banana Lollies

What do I need?

Ingredients	Utensils
2 bananas	4 wooden lolly sticks
4 large strawberries	knife
100 g natural yoghurt	spoon
200 g dark chocolate	baking tray
1 tbsp. hundreds and	freezer
thousands	microwave
	plate
	jug

What do I do? (method)

Step 1: Peel the bananas and chop each into four chunks.

Step 2: Thread a strawberry onto each lolly stick, then push on the pieces of banana.

Step 3: When all of your banana pops are made, lay them **uncovered** on a baking tray and place in the freezer for one hour.

Step 4: Pour the yoghurt into a jug and then dip each banana pop into the yoghurt to **coat** it (avoiding the strawberries). Place back onto the tray to refreeze until set.

Step 5: Melt the chocolate in the microwave and stir.

Step 6: Dip the end of each banana pop in the chocolate and then sprinkle with hundreds and thousands.

I could eat these every day! Just don't go overboard with the hundreds and thousands!

Incredible Edible Facts

Bananas float in water. They are **classified** as a berry. The inside of a banana skin can help to relieve itchy skin.

Bacon-stuffed Spuds

What do I need?

Ingredients	Utensils
4 large baking potatoes	fork
4 rashers	spoons
1 large onion, very **finely** sliced	baking tray
2 garlic cloves, very finely sliced	knives
100 g cheddar cheese, grated	pan
1 red pepper, diced	oven
2 tbsp. olive oil	bowl
salt and pepper	plate

What do I do? (method)

Step 1: Wash the potatoes and prick them all over with a fork. Rub with a little olive oil and season with salt. Pop them on a baking tray and into the oven for one hour.

Step 2: Dice the rashers and fry until crispy.

Step 3: Add the onion, garlic and peppers to the pan with the rashers and cook for 10 minutes.

Step 4: Remove the spuds from the oven. Cut in half and scoop out the **flesh**. Mash it.

Step 5: Put the mash into a bowl and add everything else from the rasher pan together. Season with a **pinch** of salt and pepper.

Step 6: Fill the potato skins with the mixture and sprinkle with cheese. Pop back in the oven for 20 minutes.

So yummy! We Irish sure do love a spud!

Incredible Edible Facts

The word 'potato' comes from the Spanish word '*patata*'. Potato plants are usually **pollinated** by insects such as bumblebees. Potatoes have lots of vitamins and minerals in them.

Queen Cakes

What do I need?

Ingredients	Utensils	
175 g self-raising flour	bun tins	bowl
125 g butter or margarine (½ a block)	bun cases	electric
125 g caster sugar	tablespoon	mixer
2 tbsp. cold water	water	wooden
2 eggs	knife	spoon
	oven	wire tray

To decorate:

Chocolate spread, hundreds and thousands, sweets, whipped cream, icing sugar, cherries, raspberries or strawberries

What do I do? (method)

Step 1: Preheat the oven to 200 degrees C/gas mark 6.

Step 2: Place bun cases into bun tins.

Step 3: Put the flour, sugar, butter, eggs and water into a bowl. Beat all of the ingredients together with an electric mixer or wooden spoon until the **mixture** is smooth.

Step 4: Put **heaped** teaspoons of the mixture into each bun case.

Step 5: Place in the oven on the top shelf and bake for 15 minutes until golden brown.

Step 6: Cool on a wire tray. When cold, decorate as you like.

These are Nana Smith's treats for special occasions like my First Holy Communion, which is next month!

Incredible Edible Facts

The word 'cupcake' was first used in the late 19th **century** for cakes made from ingredients measured by the cupful.

So, there you have it! That's <u>me on a plate</u>! I hope you get to try some out and, who knows, maybe I will meet you in the Masterchef final two years from now! From here on in, it's **practise**, practise, practise. As Nana Smith always says, "<u>If at first you don't</u> **succeed**<u>, try, try and try again.</u>"

123

Peanut Butter

by Jaymie Gerard

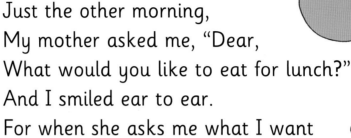

Just the other morning,
My mother asked me, "Dear,
What would you like to eat for lunch?"
And I smiled ear to ear.
For when she asks me what I want
To eat, I always say
The same delicious, nutty thing,
The same delicious way –
"Mother, I'd like peanut butter
With a drop of jam.
Or maybe on an apple, sliced,
Or diced up with some ham.
I'll take it smeared on crackers
Or mixed in with some cheese,
Or baked warm in the oven
Or frozen in the freeze'
On sandwiches, in root beer floats,
On pizza! On the floor!
Or smooshed between my fingers!
Or painted on the door!
Please, put some in the blender
And make it smooth as silk.

I don't care how you serve it, Mom –
Just don't forget the milk!"

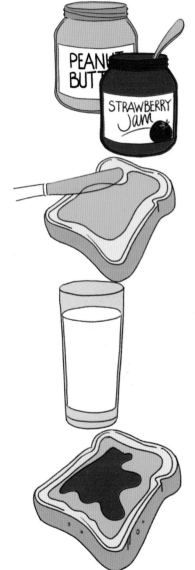

The Teachers' Surprise

My reading goal ★ Take part in and enjoy listening to reading.

It was a dewy morning in Kerrypike. The <u>birds were chirping</u>, the <u>sun was waking up</u> and the <u>flowers were blooming</u>. Tom got out of bed **sluggishly**. He looked at the calendar.

"Six more weeks until the summer holidays," he groaned.

He could hear his mam's voice inside his head: "Tom, <u>turn that frown upside down</u>!"

"OK, come on, <u>snap out of it</u>," he **grumbled**. "You can do this."

He **strummed** his guitar for a minute, wishing he could spend the day <u>rocking out some tunes</u>.

Tom's grandad had bought him the guitar for his eighth birthday and promised to get him some lessons too. But they were going to be **expensive**, so he would have to wait. <u>In the meantime</u>, he watched online lessons. Some day, he would be a rock star. Some day...

With one eye on the clock, Tom threw on his tracksuit, grabbed some toast, scrubbed his teeth and then <u>hit the road</u>.

He shuddered as <u>the cool air hit his face</u>. His dog Luna **whined** as he closed the front gate.

"I hear you," Tom said, <u>rolling his eyes</u>. "Try <u>stepping into my shoes</u>. At least you get to relax and do your own thing."

Luna looked as if she understood. She wagged her tail and watched her friend walk the short distance to Kerrypike National School.

Tom knew the route to school like the <u>back of his hand</u>. He looked down at his tracksuit as he **plodded** along. It was <u>worn at the knees</u> and stopped just above his ankles.

Suddenly, <u>a thought struck him</u>!

"Oh no! I don't think it is tracksuit day. So why did Mam leave out my tracksuit?"

He would give out to her later. She never usually got things wrong, but when she did, Tom made it known!

As he reached the school gate, something didn't seem right. Tom <u>rubbed his eyes in disbelief</u>.

"Am I seeing things?" he wondered.

This couldn't be happening. Or could it?

Ella's day got off to a great start. She woke up <u>fresh as a daisy</u> and jumped out of bed with a <u>spring in her step</u>.

She smiled as she **recalled** her dream about a fairy and a pixie who came to live in her garden. They had brought her on a magical adventure through an **enchanted** forest. She felt like Alice in Wonderland looking down into their world of little treasures.

She thought about the fairy trail she had visited at Glenview Gardens in Cork with her family at the weekend.

"That must be where my dream came from," she decided.

Ella loved fairies. She had her own fairy door in her bedroom and had actually seen a real fairy **fluttering** near it one night.

Ella **devoured** a bowl of warm porridge and gulped down a glass of freshly squeezed orange juice (with bits).

"Your uniform is wet, so you will have to wear your tracksuit today, honey. I'll write a note," her dad **announced** as she darted up the stairs.

Ella got dressed and **styled** her hair before her dad dropped her off at school.

"Bye, Dad. Love you," she **beamed**.

"Bye, love. Have a fun-filled day," her dad replied with a smirk.

As she shut the car door, Ella turned to face the school gate.

Her jaw dropped. Her eyes widened. What was going on? Was this another dream?

Ella dashed over to Tom.

"Do you see what I see?" she asked.

"Sure do," he replied.

The car park was <u>full to the brim</u> and not just with teachers' cars. There were vehicles of <u>all shapes and sizes</u> that had different **logos** printed on them. One had a picture of a bouncy castle, another of a climbing wall and another of a child in a go-kart.

As the rest of the children gathered, <u>the excitement grew</u>. Whispers of "sports day" <u>shot through the crowd</u>.

"But nobody told us," said Ella, looking **confused**.

Ella thought about her dad smirking as he had waved her off. Did he know about this?

Tom thought about his mam leaving out his tracksuit. Maybe she hadn't been wrong after all. Maybe she was in on it too!

"I think it's a surprise sports day," Ella **suggested**.

Finally, the bell rang and the teachers arrived to collect their classes. The entire school <u>erupted with laughter</u>. What stood before them was a <u>sight for sore eyes</u>! The teachers – all 27 of them – were dressed <u>from head to toe</u> as sumo wrestlers, including Mrs Lynch, the principal!

Suddenly the tune to 'Eye of the Tiger' sounded from the **intercom** speakers... do, do, do, do, do, do, do, do, do, do, do! The teachers proudly **waddled** onto the playing field. Mrs Lynch said that the day would start with a friendly sumo-wrestling contest, followed by a <u>jam-packed</u> timetable of fun-filled events. There was even going to be a hop-and-skip treasure hunt!

"Yippee!" everyone shouted.

This was going to be the best day ever!

"School isn't so bad after all," decided Tom.

Sick

by Shel Silverstein

"I cannot go to school today,"
Said little Peggy Ann McKay.
"I have the measles and the mumps,
A gash, a rash and purple bumps.
My mouth is wet, my throat is dry,
I'm going blind in my right eye.
My tonsils are as big as rocks,
I've counted sixteen chicken pox
And there's one more – that's seventeen,
And don't you think my face looks green?
My leg is cut – my eyes are blue –
It might be instamatic flu.
I cough and sneeze and gasp and choke,
I'm sure that my left leg is broke –

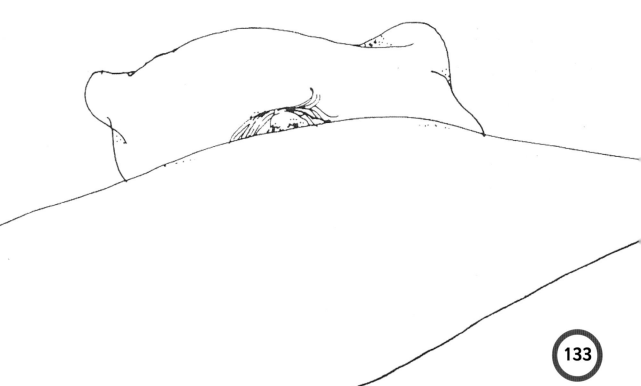

My hip hurts when I move my chin,
My belly button's caving in,
My back is wrenched, my ankle's sprained,
My 'pendix pains each time it rains.
My nose is cold, my toes are numb.
I have a sliver in my thumb.
My neck is stiff, my voice is weak,
I hardly whisper when I speak.
My tongue is filling up my mouth,
I think my hair is falling out.
My elbow's bent, my spine ain't straight,
My temperature is one-o-eight.
My brain is shrunk, I cannot hear,
There is a hole inside my ear.
I have a hangnail, and my heart is – what?
What's that? What's that you say?
You say today is... Saturday?
G'bye, I'm going out to play!"

The Day the School Stood Still

My reading goal ★ Say how punctuation and the way sentences are written help me to understand this story.

It had been raining for days. It was the kind of rain that you think is light, but it is actually a heavy **mist**. You would get <u>soaked to the bone</u> if you stepped outside. Lainey stared out the window and watched **murky** grey clouds roll by. She was used to being <u>out and about</u> and <u>on the go</u>. She was finding it hard to **occupy** herself after school in this miserable weather.

"It's so boring staying inside, Mam," she said in a fed-up voice. "I thought it never rains in May, so why is it <u>coming down in buckets</u>?"

Lainey had been like this since she first learned to talk – questions, questions, questions!

Her dad said, "She is very clever and needs to be **stimulated**."

But in her mam's opinion, "She was given too much attention as a baby, being the first born 'n' all."

135

For Lainey, every day was a wild adventure, but this rain was <u>stopping her in her tracks</u>! And things were about to get worse. Ms Carol would be leaving to have her baby on Friday and the 'newbie' would be arriving to take her place!

Lainey loved her teacher and didn't want to see her go. So far this year, Ms Carol had taught them the tin whistle, taken them on nature walks and did conversation stations, which were really cool. But now, <u>in full bloom</u>, it was time for her to go. That's it, fun's over!

The principal said that she **expected** the class to be *extra* nice to the 'newbie' and show them just what Kerrypikers were made of.

On Newbie Eve – the evening before the newbie arrived – Lainey lay <u>tossing and turning</u> in her bed. What would her new teacher be like?

Would she be a lady like Ms Honey from *Matilda*, whom she could call Ms Rose Petal? Or would he be a man with a beard, whom she could call Mr Beardface? Would she give them golden time? Would he give them <u>mountains of homework</u>?

And off she went again – questions, questions, questions!

On Friday, Lainey was sitting at the red table with Jenna, Michael and Callum. There was no sign of the newbie yet and everyone was **yapping** and joking. Lainey was <u>on the edge of her seat</u>, tapping her pencil against the table. The noise **barometer** was <u>through the roof</u>! Then, silence.

Everyone's jaw dropped. Aoife pointed. Daniel **gasped**. Jessica cried. Was this really the newbie? Surely this was just a joke and their *real* teacher would come walking through the door any minute, right? Wrong.

From that moment on, the lives of these Second Class pupils were changed and going to school would never be the same again. From that moment on, **unusual** things would start happening.

"What was the matter?" you ask. "What was wrong with the newbie?" Come, dear reader and let me tell you all about Ms Grant, or should I say, *Witch* Grant!

You probably think you already know all there is to know about witches, but you don't. You might think that they're not even real, but you're wrong. If you're going to be in on this, you need to <u>wise up</u>, and be **alert** to the facts.

Sure, you've seen them on TV. You might have dressed up as one at Hallowe'en. You've read the *Winnie the Witch* books and watched *The Wizard of Oz*. Picture a wart-nosed, ugly, old woman wearing a black **ragged** dress and riding a broom. That's a witch, right? Imagine a spell-casting, pointy-hat wearing, black-cat owning **cackler**. That's a witch, right? If you think that's it, think again.

The next bit might surprise you, but I'm telling you this for your own good. Who knows if there are more witch teachers out there? What follows is a list of the **traits** of **modern-day** witch teachers. These are the things that you need to look out for.

1. They look like normal people, without ugly, warty faces or **withered** skin. Their hair is nicely styled, their nails are **manicured** and they even have a rosy-cheeked glow.

2. They wear funky trainers. They try to blend in and look **hip**. They wear the latest **trends** and always look, dare we say it, cool.

3. They use social media. You might catch them at break time, **uploading** a live chat or laughing with one of the other teachers at their emoji faces. Don't be fooled. They are up to something.

4. They hate lunchtime supervision. You will hear them <u>mumble and grumble</u> an unusual chant under their breath. If there's anything that <u>gets their goat</u>, it's trying to watch over wild children while trying to **digest** a sandwich that they've eaten in a single gulp.

5. They're always writing notes to other teachers and carrying piles of books. What could they possibly be writing and why do they need *soooo* many books? ("Spells?" I hear you say.)

6. Their lunches always look super healthy. Five a day ✓ – check! I guess they're saving the **poisonous** treats for us.

7. They drive a family car. What is that about? Do they not just live at school? Or maybe it's for taking pupils home in!

It's not as **obvious** as you thought, right? So, how can you ever hope to tell a real teacher from a witch teacher? Here's how (and this is how we knew that Ms Grant was one the very first time we laid eyes on her):

8. Take a deep breath, my friend, for the words I'm about to say are true: THEY HAVE EYES AT THE BACK OF THEIR HEADS!

Saw My Teacher on a Saturday

by Dave Crawley

Saw my teacher on a Saturday!
I can't believe it's true!
I saw her buying groceries,
like normal people do!

She reached for bread and turned around,
and then she caught my eye.
She gave a smile and said, "Hello."
I thought that I would die!

"Oh, hi... hello, Miss Appleton,"
I mumbled like a fool.
I guess I thought that teacher types
spend all their time at school.

To make the situation worse,
my mom was at my side.
So many rows of jars and cans.
So little room to hide.

Oh please, I thought, don't tell my mom
what I did yesterday!
I closed my eyes and held my breath
and hoped she'd go away.

Some people think it's fine to let
our teachers walk about.
But when it comes to Saturdays,
they shouldn't let them out!

The Mysterious House

My reading goal ★ Use word attack strategies to solve new words.

It was <u>a scorcher of a day</u>. <u>The sun was splitting the stones</u>. The sky was blue, with not a whisper of cloud. It was still a couple of hours until midday but it was already **sweltering**.

Little **droplets** of sweat were gathering on Tom's neck and behind his knees. He was playing ball. He flicked the ball into the air to try and break his record of 'keepie-uppies'.

He started off well, bouncing the ball from his knee to his foot and back again. However, he always started to wobble at 15 and today was no different.

He watched, <u>in slow motion</u>, as the ball **sailed** over the hedge of Miss Teary's house, before landing in her garden.

"Oh no," thought Tom, "Miss Teary will kill me!"

Miss Teary's garden was not a place where children wanted to go. It was surrounded by laurel hedging. The grass was wild and long. The house was so **rundown** that it looked as if a strong wind could blow it down.

However, it wasn't the gloomy house that scared the local children. It was its **resident**! Miss Teary was an **elderly** woman who spent all day, every day gazing out her bedroom window. Wherever you went on the street, if you looked up to her window, her eyes were on you. She never left the window for a second during the day. It seemed like she never ate, went to the toilet or watched TV. Nothing!

Miss Teary was **ancient**. Her face was very crinkly, like someone had taken a photo of the world's oldest person and squashed it tight before unfolding the paper – so deep were her wrinkles.

Some said that she was a witch. Others said that she was a ghost. Whatever she was, she was not nice at all! It had been nearly two years since the last child had **dared** to enter her garden. Evan had gone in to **retrieve** a frisbee and Miss Teary <u>went bananas</u>! You could hear her screaming from miles away.

If it were any other ball, Tom would be **tempted** to leave it, but this ball was new. Also, it was the type that they use in the Champions League.

Slowly, Tom trudged over to the house and placed his **trembling** hand on the old wooden gate. He looked up to see if Miss Teary was watching, but her bedroom window was hidden from view by the laurel bush. He knew she had seen, though. He could feel her eyes on him.

He tiptoed through the gate and scanned the garden. There, by a **gnarled** tree, was his ball. He began sprinting to the ball. The quicker he got it, the quicker he would be out. He had taken only a few **strides** when he heard the screaming of a **banshee**.

"Stop, stop, boy! Don't move or I will get you!" Tom heard someone shout.

He froze, <u>standing as still as a statue</u>.

"<u>Do not move a muscle</u>," said Miss Teary as she ran over.

Despite being at least 150 years old, she was <u>as fast as a greyhound</u>. Within seconds, she was upon him. Tom closed his eyes, waiting to be turned into a frog, a slug or another slimy creature. He **braced** himself, but nothing came.

He slowly raised his eyelids and saw that Miss Teary was kneeling near his feet, gently **caressing** the grass with her hands.

"Are you OK? Is everyone safe?" she asked in a worried voice. "... 17, 18, 19, 20... oh, thank goodness, you are all there."

As Tom **strained** his eyes to look at the ground, he could make out something moving in the long grass. What he saw took his breath away. There in the grass was a row of tiny houses, slightly bigger than matchboxes. Tiny **wisps** of smoke piped from the chimneys and **faint** lights shone from the windows. In front of the houses was a street. It was **hustling** and **bustling** with activity. Little people with wings were busy going about their business.

"Are they… fairies?" asked Tom with surprise.

"Yes, they are," replied Miss Teary <u>with a twinkle in her eye</u>. "They've been living here on the lawn for the past 15 years. I came out one day to cut the grass and there they were. I almost **destroyed** their street with my lawnmower and since then I've promised to protect them."

"So that's why you are always looking out your window?" **quizzed** Tom.

"Yes it is. I know that <u>kids will be kids</u>, but balls coming into the garden and children **plodding** in after them could wipe out the whole fairy village! I don't like shouting and scaring the neighbourhood children, but what other choice do I have?"

"It must be lonely, staying in by yourself to mind the fairies," he **remarked**.

"It is, but I can't let anything happen to them," said Miss Teary. "They're my family."

Miss Teary <u>looked as sad and as lonely as a goldfish in a bowl</u>.

"Tom, you're the first person to find out my secret. If anyone were to find out, the fairies' lives would be in danger," Miss Teary said.

"I won't say a word," said Tom. "But can I come and visit them, and you too of course?"

Miss Teary looked at Tom for a while, studying his face with her **keen** eyes. Then she broke out into a smile.

"That would be lovely. I could do with all the help I can get and having a visitor would be nice," she said. "Look, why don't you come back tomorrow and I can **introduce** you to the fairies? I'll even bake a cake for us."

Tom smiled. "I can't wait," he said.

After all the years of fearing the mysterious house and the dreaded Miss Teary, Tom realised that <u>things are not always as they seem</u>.

If You See a Fairy Ring
by William Shakespeare

If you see a fairy ring

In a field of grass,

Very lightly step around,

Tiptoe as you pass.

Last night fairies frolicked there,

And they're sleeping somewhere near.

If you see a tiny fay

Lying fast asleep,

Shut your eyes and run away,

Do not stay or peep.

And be sure you never tell,

Or you'll break a fairy spell.